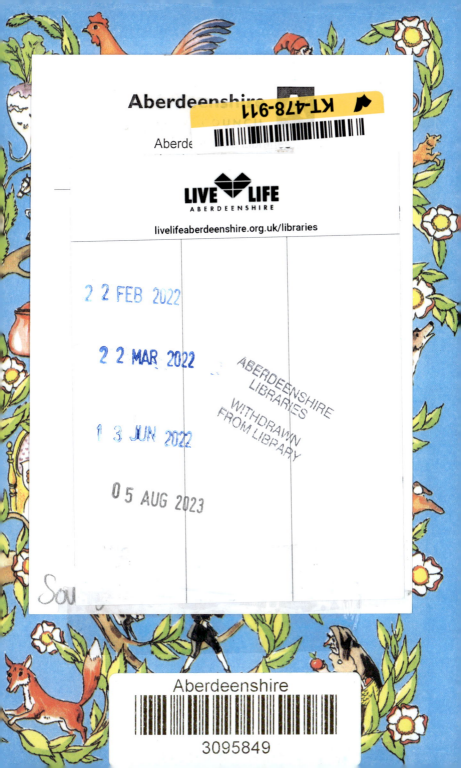

This *LADYBIRD TALE*
belongs to

....

Beauty
and the Beast

Retold by Vera Southgate M.A., B.COM
with illustrations by Yunhee Park

LADYBIRD TALES

ONCE UPON A TIME, in a town far away, there lived a rich merchant who had three pretty daughters.

The youngest daughter was the prettiest of the three and she was called Beauty. She was as good and kind as she was lovely. Her elder sisters, although they too were pretty, were neither kind nor good. They were selfish and proud.

One day their father came home looking very grave. When his daughters asked him what was the matter, he replied, "Alas, I am no longer rich. I have lost my fortune. We must all leave this beautiful house and go to live in a cottage in the country."

The elder sisters were very angry when they learned this news.

"What shall we do with ourselves all day in the country?" they asked.

Beauty said, "How nice it will be to live in the country among the woods and fields and flowers."

So their father found a little cottage with a large garden in the country, and they all went to live there.

The father worked hard in the garden and, by selling his fruit and vegetables, made enough money to live comfortably.

One day, the father gathered his three daughters together and told them that he had to go to a distant town, on business. He might not return until the next day.

"Is there any little gift which I might bring home for you?" he asked each of his daughters in turn.

"Diamonds for me," said the eldest daughter.

"Pearls for me," said the second daughter.

"Please, Father, a bunch of white roses for me," said Beauty.

Then their father rode away on horseback and Beauty waved to him from the doorstep.

When the merchant had finished his business he set off for home. Before long it grew dark and he lost his way. He found himself in a dense wood and could find no way out.

Then, at last, he saw a light in the distance and he rode towards it. However, as he drew nearer to the light, he found that the trees formed a wide avenue. He rode up the avenue and, to his surprise, arrived at the entrance to a palace.

The door of the palace stood open, but there was no one in sight so the merchant walked in. He went into a room on the right of the hall, where a fire blazed in the hearth. There he found a table set with supper for one.